J 70876

2008-1
2005-2

Raintree - Steck - Vaughn 4/92

Raintree
20.00

Old Slippery

Story by Mark Belanger
Illustrations by Shirley V. Beckes

RAINTREE
STECK-VAUGHN
L I B R A R Y

Austin, Texas

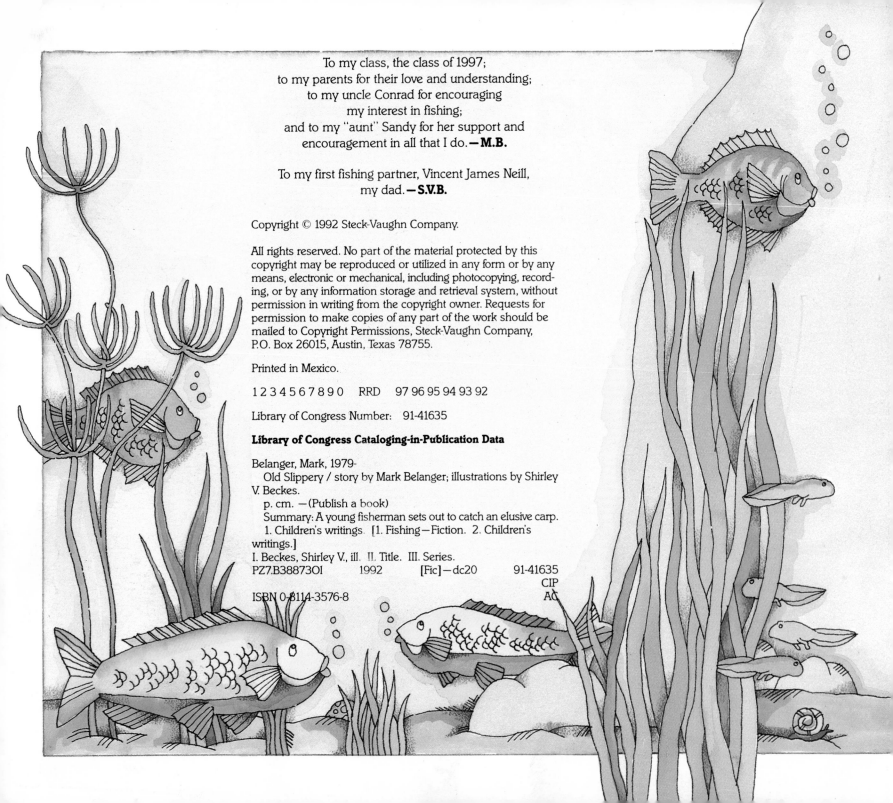

To my class, the class of 1997;
to my parents for their love and understanding;
to my uncle Conrad for encouraging
my interest in fishing;
and to my "aunt" Sandy for her support and
encouragement in all that I do. — **M.B.**

To my first fishing partner, Vincent James Neill,
my dad. — **S.V.B.**

Printed in Mexico.

1 2 3 4 5 6 7 8 9 0   RRD   97 96 95 94 93 92

Library of Congress Number: 91-41635

Library of Congress Cataloging-in-Publication Data

Belanger, Mark, 1979-
    Old Slippery / story by Mark Belanger; illustrations by Shirley V. Beckes.
    p. cm. —(Publish a book)
    Summary: A young fisherman sets out to catch an elusive carp.
    1. Children's writings. [1. Fishing—Fiction. 2. Children's writings.]
I. Beckes, Shirley V., ill. II. Title. III. Series.
PZ7.B388730I   1992   [Fic]—dc20   91-41635
                                                                        CIP
                                                                        AC
ISBN 0-8114-3576-8

It was five-thirty when the alarm buzzed. I jumped out of bed, dressing as fast as I could in my jeans, T-shirt, and favorite old sneakers. I ate breakfast and packed my lunch—a large peanut butter sandwich, a box of grape juice, and three chocolate chip cookies—in a small cooler. In a separate jug, I put some ice and water.

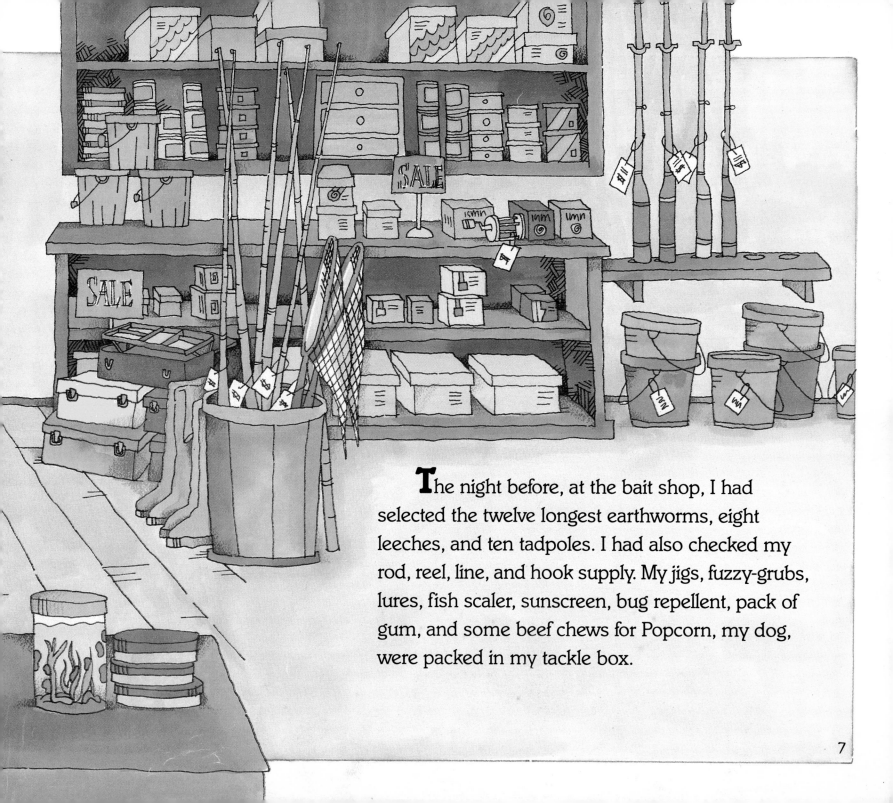

The night before, at the bait shop, I had selected the twelve longest earthworms, eight leeches, and ten tadpoles. I had also checked my rod, reel, line, and hook supply. My jigs, fuzzy-grubs, lures, fish scaler, sunscreen, bug repellent, pack of gum, and some beef chews for Popcorn, my dog, were packed in my tackle box.

Picking up my lunch cooler, I went to the garage. After transferring my bait to my tackle box, I picked up my pole and gear and started up the hill. Popcorn trotted at my heels.

My big adventure had begun. Today I was determined to catch Old Slippery, the big carp in the pond. For two summers I had tried to catch this sneaky fish. I wasn't the only one to try. People from all over our area had been after him for years. As far as I knew, he was older than me.

11

When I first saw him two years ago, leaping in the center of the pond, I was on a campout with my Boy Scout troop. I foolishly vowed that day that I would be the one to finally hook the monster. After two years I was no closer to my goal. I was desperate. I was tired of being teased about Old Slippery. I would catch him this time if it took all day and all night. I planned to take him to the Boy Scout picnic Thursday and show everyone.

13

Heading for my favorite old tree stump, I circled the pond and crossed the fallen log bridge. Popcorn followed, splashing through the water at the pond's edge. When I reached the stump, I set down my gear and walked along the water's edge. Sometimes Old Slippery hid in the rocks and shadows.

15

I opened my bait box and picked the largest leech for my hook. I cast the line and settled down to wait. Sitting there I remembered the day two summers ago when I had hooked Old Slippery. As I reeled him in, my line had snapped, and he slipped away. After that, I always used thirty-pound line.

16

Two hours later I stopped to get a drink and
eat a cookie. When I looked across the pond, I saw
Old Slippery jumping about twenty feet from shore.
He seemed to be teasing me.

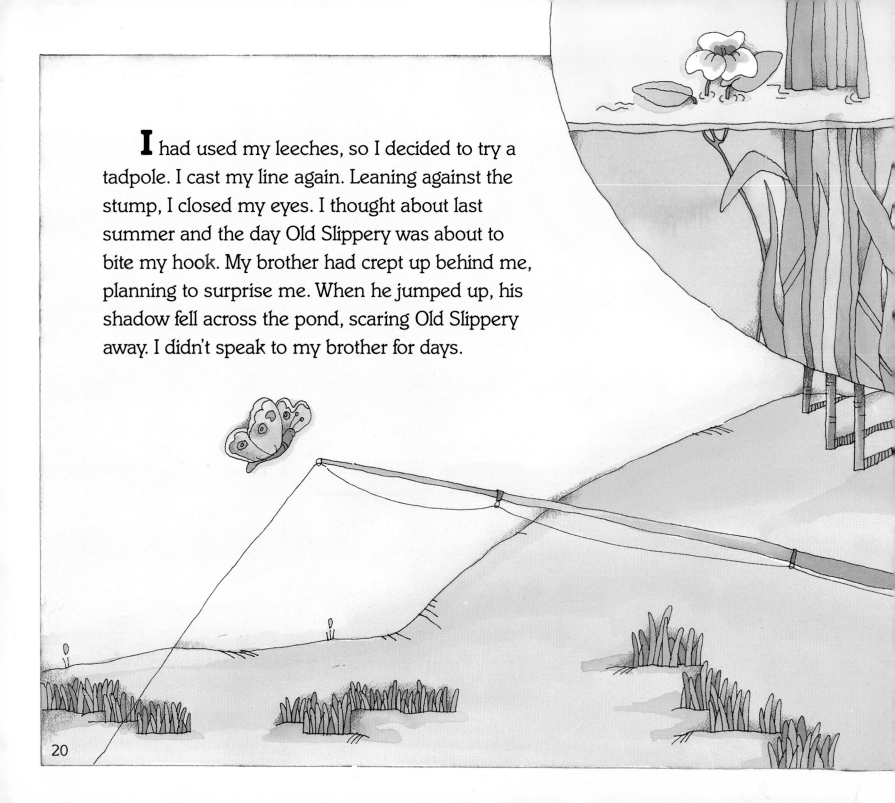

I had used my leeches, so I decided to try a tadpole. I cast my line again. Leaning against the stump, I closed my eyes. I thought about last summer and the day Old Slippery was about to bite my hook. My brother had crept up behind me, planning to surprise me. When he jumped up, his shadow fell across the pond, scaring Old Slippery away. I didn't speak to my brother for days.

By the time I stopped for lunch, the tadpoles and half of the earthworms were gone. I had caught and thrown back two sunfish, one bluegill, and a bass. All I wanted was Old Slippery. Once my earthworms were gone, I started using fuzzy-grubs. There was no sign of Old Slippery.

At four o'clock my mother drove to the top of the hill and yelled that I had one more hour to fish. I was tired, hungry, and discouraged. But I wasn't ready to give up yet. As I ate one of my two remaining cookies, it broke and a piece fell on the ground. I picked it up and threw it into the pond. As soon as it hit the water, Old Slippery swam into the shallows and ate it. I broke my last cookie and dropped a piece in the water. Old Slippery struck again. I had discovered his weakness—cookies.

I put a piece of cookie on my hook and dropped it gently into the shallow water. Old Slippery swam in. He was hooked! I quickly flipped him onto the bank. As I looked down at him flopping about, the hook still in his mouth, I saw that his body was badly scarred. He was an old fish and weighed about eighteen pounds. He had stopped moving and he was watching me. He knew his fate was in my hands.

I reached down and held him still as I carefully removed the hook. Picking him up, I gently slipped him back into the water. He hesitated a moment, then swam away.

28

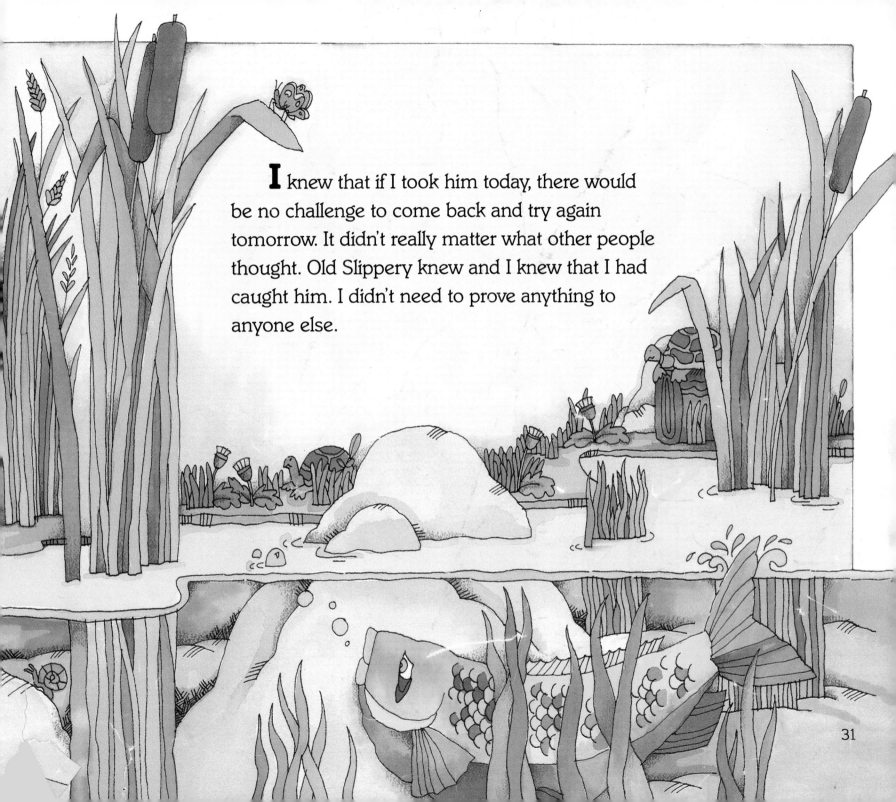

I knew that if I took him today, there would be no challenge to come back and try again tomorrow. It didn't really matter what other people thought. Old Slippery knew and I knew that I had caught him. I didn't need to prove anything to anyone else.

Mark Belanger, the twelve-year-old author of **Old Slippery**, wrote the story when he was in the sixth grade at Wayland Central School in Wayland, New York. As a member of SHARE, a program for gifted students, Mark was sponsored in the Publish-a-Book contest by Ruth Ann Hayward, the local SHARE coordinator.

Mark lives with his parents, Gary and Donna, and his older brother, Jason, on eleven acres of land just outside the village of Wayland, New York. Wayland is about fifty miles south of Rochester and is in the heart of the Finger Lakes farming country. Mark's father is employed at Eastman Kodak and is active in the U.S. Army Reserves. His mother is a registered nurse.

Mark loves the outdoors and all types of animals. His home provides ample opportunity for hunting, fishing, exploring, and collecting snakes, frogs, and other small animals. Mark and his family have numerous pets. Popcorn, his dog, is mentioned in **Old Slippery**. There are also cats, rabbits, guinea pigs, and a registered quarterhorse named Cody Cheyenne.

The pond in **Old Slippery** is real. It is located on the hill behind Mark's house. Mark's interest in fishing and hunting is shared by his brother and encouraged by his uncle Conrad, an avid hunter and fisherman. Mark decided to write about fishing because he has been encouraged to write about what he knows and likes to do.

Mark also enjoys biking and horseback riding. He plays soccer in a summer league and Little League baseball. He has been a member of the Wayland Wrestling Club and the Boy Scouts. Although Mark is not exactly sure what he wants to do after high school, he is interested in the criminal justice field and in veterinary medicine. Whatever he does, he will continue to enjoy fishing.

The twenty honorable-mention winners in the **1991 Raintree/Steck-Vaughn Publish-a-Book Contest** were Wendy Leigh Bleyl of Houston, Texas; Sybrina Brantley of Crossett, Arkansas; Katie Drury of Troy, Michigan; Brittany Erkman of Annapolis, Maryland; Laura Jagusch of Dearborn Heights, Michigan; Nathan Knell of Duncanville, Texas; Jeremy Mistretta of Houston, Texas; Matthew Moffa of Ligonier, Pennsylvania; Amy Nawatka of South Milwaukee, Wisconsin; Pamela Parris of New Hampshire; Katie Reinart of Cincinnati, Ohio; Lori Scrudato of Bayonne, New Jersey; Cam Sele of Fairbanks, Alaska; Jennifer Shaffer of Weatherford, Oklahoma; Nicole Shiraishi of Kailua, Hawaii; Tori Smith of Walkerton, Indiana; W. Destin Veach-Cook of Duncanville, Texas; Jaclyn Webb of Moore, Oklahoma; Laurie Winston of Milford, Connecticut; and Amanda Lee Yeager of Belle, West Virginia.

Shirley V. Beckes was born Shirley Virginia Neill in Columbus, Ohio. After graduating from Columbus College of Art and Design in 1965, she moved to Chicago, Illinois. Since 1979, Shirley and her husband, David, have lived in Milwaukee, Wisconsin, where they maintain their studio, Beckes Design/Illustration.